DATE DUE

BONEYARD

Janet Lorimer

PAGETURNERS

SUSPENSE

Boneyard
The Cold, Cold Shoulder
The Girl Who Had Everything
Hamlet's Trap
Roses Red as Blood

ADVENTURE

A Horse Called Courage
Planet Doom
The Terrible Orchid Sky
Up Rattler Mountain
Who Has Seen the Beast?

MYSTERY

The Hunter
Once Upon a Crime
Whatever Happened to
  Megan Marie?
When Sleeping Dogs Awaken
Where's Dudley?

DETECTIVE

The Case of the Bad Seed
The Case of the Cursed Chalet
The Case of the Dead Duck
The Case of the Wanted Man
The Case of the Watery Grave

SCIENCE FICTION

Bugged!
Escape from Earth
Flashback
Murray's Nightmare
Under Siege

SPY

A Deadly Game
An Eye for an Eye
I Spy, e-Spy
Scavenger Hunt
Tuesday Raven

Development and Production: Laurel Associates, Inc.
Cover and Interior Art: Black Eagle Productions

SADDLEBACK
PUBLISHING·INC.
Three Watson
Irvine, CA 92618-2767
E-Mail: info@sdlback.com
Website: www.sdlback.com

ISBN 1-56254-700-3

Printed in the United States of America

09 08 07 06   9 8 7 6 5 4 3 2 1

CONTENTS

Chapter 1

Wilma Roberts parked her car at the top of the bluff and got out. For a moment she stood quietly staring out across the ocean. Today the surf was smooth. Blue water mirrored blue sky, and gentle waves broke into creamy foam on the shore. Seagulls swooped overhead, their cries breaking the silence.

She thought about other times she'd stood here—times when it was stormy, or nights when the moon was full. She thought about the bloody battle that had been fought on the beach 200 years ago.

She remembered things she'd seen and sounds she'd heard there—strange sights and sounds she couldn't explain. Wilma shivered. She loved Wreckers Cove, but sometimes it was just a little *too* spooky.

Every time I stand on this bluff, I feel like I've gone back in time, Wilma thought. *There's so much history here. Too bad it's about to be destroyed.*

She glared at the new sign that had just been posted at the top of the bluff.

Welcome to Wreckers Cove
Future Site of the Wreckers Cove Resort!
Another Project of Jolly Roger Enterprises!

Jolly Roger Enterprises was the company owned by Roger Anderson, a local land developer. He claimed to have the town's best interests at heart—but Wilma wasn't so sure. Her hometown was becoming nothing but a tourist trap.

Tomorrow morning heavy equipment and noisy construction workers would be all over this place. Within a few months, the resort would block the public view. Local people wouldn't be able to get down to the cove. Roger planned to keep the cove for his paying customers.

I sure hope the local people agree that

it was worth it, Wilma thought sadly.

The sound of laughter and shouts broke through her thoughts. Wilma glanced over her shoulder. Two boys were running toward the path that led down to the beach. One of the teenagers was tall with dark hair. He was carrying a couple of boogie boards. Wilma recognized him at once. He was Steve, Roger Anderson's son.

Running behind him was a smaller boy with blond hair. He was loaded down with towels, water bottles, and sunscreen. Wilma had never seen him before. *He must be a newcomer,* she thought.

The tall boy plunged down the steep path. The blond-haired boy slowed and stopped. Roger Anderson's sign had caught his attention. "Hey, Steve," he called out to his friend, "why is this place called Wreckers Cove?"

Steve didn't stop or glance back. "Who cares?" he yelled over his shoulder. "Maybe there used to be an auto wrecking yard here or something. Come on, Donny, the waves look perfect."

Donny frowned. "An auto wrecking yard?" he muttered. "Right on the beach? That's dumb!"

"And wrong," Wilma said. She couldn't help herself. The history of this town was important to her. She didn't often have a chance to talk about it.

Donny glanced at Wilma, noticing her for the first time. "What do you mean?"

"The town of Wreckers Cove is named after this place," Wilma said. Then she smiled and introduced herself. "I happen to love history," she added.

Donny smiled back. "Me, too," the boy said, as he shook her hand.

Then he asked, "But you still haven't told me what a 'wrecker' is."

Wilma pointed down at the beach. "See how protected the cove looks?"

Donny nodded.

"It's not really a safe place," Wilma said. "Just a few hundred yards out in the ocean, there's a nasty reef. Steep rocks rise up under the water. Some of them are as sharp as shark's teeth."

Donny frowned. "So?"

"The Wreckers were people who lived in this area about 200 years ago," Wilma explained. "At one time they had been smugglers. Then they decided to stay here and lure ships onto the reef. In those days, the wooden ships easily broke up on the rocks. That's where the word 'Wreckers' comes from. First the Wreckers wrecked the ships. Then they stole the cargo."

"Wow!" Donny said. "So they were really like pirates."

Wilma nodded.

"Hey, Donny!" Steve was already on his boogie board. He sounded impatient.

Donny sighed. "I guess I'd better get down there," he said. "But I'd really like to hear more about those Wreckers."

"I'll walk with you," Wilma said. "I love the beach this time of day."

When they reached the sand, Donny

spread out a towel and they sat down.

Steve hadn't waited around. He was already paddling out to meet the waves.

"What kind of cargo did the smugglers get?" Donny asked.

"All kinds of things," Wilma said. "Silk and lace. Fine china. Gold coins."

"What about the people on the ships? What happened to the sailors and the passengers?" Donny asked.

"Well, that's the ugly part of our town's history," Wilma said. "Some of the people drowned when the ships smashed on the rocks. But the Wreckers couldn't afford to leave any witnesses. They made sure that any survivors never made it off the beach."

Donny's eyes widened. "You mean they *murdered* the rest of the people?"

Wilma nodded. "They sure did. The Wreckers murdered a lot of innocent people to cover up their crimes."

"Wow, what a story!" Donny said. "How long did this go on? Someone must have gotten suspicious after a while."

"Oh, sure, there were plenty of complaints," Wilma said. "But remember that news traveled slowly in those days. No telephones, no e-mail!"

Donny laughed.

"Finally, the governor realized there was a problem," Wilma went on. "He sent the militia to Wreckers Cove. The soldiers found stolen cargo hidden in people's homes and barns. Right here on this beach there was a bloody battle between the soldiers and the Wreckers."

"Who won?" Donny asked.

"The soldiers, of course," Wilma said. "In fact, most of the Wreckers were killed that day. People say that on stormy nights here at the cove, you can still hear their ghosts wailing and moaning."

Chapter 2

Donny grinned. "I love ghost stories!" he exclaimed. "Of course I don't *really* believe in ghosts," he added. "Do you?"

Wilma was tempted to tell Donny about the times she'd come down to the beach at night and heard—

"Hey, Donny. Are you coming in?" Steve's yell cut into Wilma's thoughts.

Steve was paddling toward them on his boogie board. He looked very annoyed.

"I guess I'd better go," Donny said. "Steve's been begging me to go boogie boarding for a week—ever since I got here. And pretty soon, we won't be able to come here at all."

"Are you and Steve friends from school?" Wilma asked.

"Cousins," Donny told her. "I'm here for the summer. Steve and Uncle Roger haven't told me much about the history of this place. But I sure would like to hear more about those Wreckers."

"Did you ever read 'A Smugglers' Song'?" Wilma asked.

Donny shook his head.

"It's a poem written by Rudyard Kipling," Wilma explained. "The voice of an adult is warning a little girl to be quiet if she hears smugglers at night. I used to know it by heart, but I'm not sure I remember all of it now."

She frowned a moment, and then she began to quote:

"If you wake at midnight, and hear a horse's feet,

Don't go drawing back the blind, or looking in the street,

Them that asks no questions isn't told a lie.

Watch the wall, my darling, while the Gentlemen go by!"

"I guess the Gentlemen were the smugglers," Donny said.

Wilma nodded. "A lot of people around here still tell stories about the Wreckers—tales passed down from their great-grandparents. In fact most people in this area are actually descended from Wreckers."

"Wow!" Donny looked impressed. "Are you?"

"Yeah. According to family history, one of my ancestors was a smuggler."

"Cool," Donny said.

"But don't forget," Wilma went on, "that the Wreckers were thieves and murderers. I don't think their victims thought they were very cool."

Donny laughed. Then a sudden ringing interrupted the mood. Wilma pulled her cell phone from her pocket and took the call. As she hung up, she said, "Now it's my turn! I have to get going. My boss wants me!"

"What do you do?" Donny asked.

"I'm a reporter," Wilma said. She handed Donny one of her business cards. "Look, if you want to talk some more, give me a call. I was born and raised here. I've heard enough Wrecker stories to write a book." She started for the path, then turned back. "If the weather gets much hotter, I'll tell you some ghost stories that'll send chills up your spine."

On her way back to town, Wilma's thoughts turned from the Wreckers to Roger Anderson. In his own way, Roger reminded Wilma of a Wrecker. He didn't lure ships onto rocks, but he certainly lured a lot of tourists into the area.

"Not like that's a *bad* thing," she told herself. "It brings money to the town. I just don't like the pushy way that Roger does things."

Roger had convinced local people that the town's bloody history could attract visitors. The City Council agreed. They let Jolly Roger Enterprises have its way.

Roger began by building a museum

on Main Street. He called it the Museum of the Macabre, and he'd chosen to display every gruesome event from the town's history there. Wilma had toured the museum a time or two. She had to admit it seemed to be popular.

Roger's next project was a restaurant called The Crow's Nest. The interior was decorated to look like an old sailing ship. Big fishnets and ships' anchors hung on the walls. The waiters were dressed like pirates, and the menu featured items like Smuggler Salads and Buccaneer Burgers. The whole thing was pretty corny, but visitors loved it.

The trouble is, Wilma thought as she drove, *there's more to Wreckers Cove than the Wreckers. There were some very good people who lived here, too. Some of those folks did wonderful things for the town. It's too bad no one wants to remember* them.

Now Roger was ready to build the resort at the cove. And after that, he planned to build an amusement park south of town. Wilma sighed. "What will be next?" she wondered.

She had just pulled up into the newspaper building's parking lot when her cell phone rang again.

"Where are you?" her boss grumbled. Mel Fisher was the editor of the *Wreckers Cove Gazette*. He'd moved to this area five years ago. As far as local people were concerned, Mel was still a newcomer and always would be.

"If you look out your window, you'll see me," Wilma told Mel, as she climbed out of her car and waved.

"Good thing," Mel snapped. "I've got a woman here waiting for you. She has something to say about the site of that new resort!"

# Chapter 3

The woman in Mel's office turned out to be Audrey Cain. Wilma had known her for years. Right now she was sitting on a chair in front of Mel's desk, looking a little nervous.

"Audrey and I know each other," Wilma told Mel when he tried to introduce them. "We went to the same high school. Audrey was a couple of years ahead of me."

"I keep forgetting that you grew up here," Mel grunted at Wilma. He turned to Audrey. "Okay. Go ahead and tell Wilma what you told me about the cove."

"My family has lived here for generations," Audrey said, looking straight at Mel. She spoke with a soft Southern drawl. "The story I'm telling you has come down to me through the family. And I believe it's true."

She twisted her hands together. "I guess you already know that all of us Cains are descended from Jack Cain, one of the Wreckers."

Wilma nodded. She noticed that Audrey didn't add that Jack's nickname had been "Bloody Jack." Why? Because he'd murdered his victims with a single knife slice across the jugular vein. Bloody and effective.

"The story goes that during the battle at the cove, Jack Cain was the last to die," Audrey said. She looked from Mel to Wilma to see if they were impressed. "The captain of the militia clubbed Jack to death. As he lay dying, they say that he put a curse on the beach."

"Go on," Mel said, trying to hide his impatience. Wilma smiled. It took a lot to impress Mel Fisher.

"Jack warned the soldiers that people would pay for any blood they had spilled on the sand," Audrey went on.

Wilma noticed that Audrey was making her story sound overly dramatic.

"I've heard that story," Wilma said. "But people have been going to the cove to swim and picnic for years. Nothing unusual has ever happened there."

Audrey frowned at Wilma. "Roger Anderson is going to hurt a lot of people by building on the cove," she said. "He's going to stir up old trouble."

"What trouble?" Mel asked.

"Oh, I don't know exactly what's going to happen," Audrey said. "All I'm doing is passing on the warning."

She licked her thin lips nervously and gazed at Mel. "I think you should put that story in the paper. Your readers need to be warned."

"Wilma is the one writing all the articles about the resort," Mel said. He grinned at Wilma as if to say, "Okay, now it's your problem." Out loud he said, "What do you think, Wil?"

"I think we could probably use some of the story as background color," Wilma agreed. "The old-timers in town would enjoy it. But we have a lot of newcomers in Wreckers Cove now. I sure wouldn't want to start a panic."

Mel nodded. "I agree. And there must be other legends you could use, too."

Audrey licked her thin lips again. "So how much are you going to pay me for my story?" she asked.

Wilma tried to hide a smile. Now she realized why Audrey had seemed to be so nervous.

Mel shook his head. "Sorry, but the paper doesn't pay for information."

Audrey started to protest. But Mel added, "We will certainly mention your name in the article, Ms. Cain."

Audrey was annoyed. "*Humph!*" she said over her shoulder as she stomped out of Mel's office.

"Thanks a lot," Wilma said to her boss. "You sure put me on the spot."

Mel grinned at her. "Had you heard her story before?" he asked.

Wilma nodded. "It's part of the history of the Battle of Wreckers Cove." Then Wilma told Mel about Bloody Jack Cain. "Many of his descendants are proud that he was such a cold-hearted killer. But as far as I'm concerned, the man was just another scummy criminal."

Mel laughed. "Tomorrow's the big day when the bulldozers start to roll. Having Jack Cain's warning on page one might be kind of interesting."

Wilma groaned. "I know you dislike Roger Anderson," she said. "But do you really think that story is a good idea?"

"Probably not," Mel said with a smirk. "But let's run it anyway."

The next morning Wilma stopped at the news building before heading to the cove. "I thought I'd see what's going on down there," she told Mel. "And I need a photographer. Is anyone free?"

"I just sent a guy down to the cove to

get some pictures," Mel said. "By the way, Wil, your story about Jack Cain was terrific! Everyone loved it! The phones are ringing off the hook."

"That's good," Wilma said as she stood and headed for the door.

"Be sure to let me know if anything strange happens down at the cove," Mel called after her.

"You want me to try to get an interview with the ghost of Bloody Jack Cain?" Wilma asked jokingly.

"If you do, we'll run it on page one—and you'll get a raise," Mel called out with a loud guffaw.

Wilma couldn't help smiling. "Thanks for nothing," she said.

She reached the cove a few minutes later. As she parked her car, she was surprised to see a couple of police cars nearby. Their lights were flashing.

Traffic control? Wilma wondered as she got out of her car.

All of a sudden she was struck by the

silence. She saw that a crowd had gathered on the bluff. She heard voices, but she didn't hear any bulldozers. And no dust clouds spiraled into the air.

Wilma headed for the crowd. She had a bad feeling that something had gone very, very wrong. Had someone had an accident?

A ribbon of yellow crime-scene tape stopped her at the edge of the crowd. Everyone was staring at a group of cops and construction workers who were studying something on the ground.

"What's going on?" Wilma asked the man standing next to her.

"The workers had just started digging," he said excitedly. "Almost immediately they brought up bones— human bones."

Chapter 4

As Wilma watched, one of the workers yelled, "Hey! Over here. I found another one." He held up a human skull.

Wilma saw a gaping hole in the side of the skull. Did that happen *after* the person had died—or did it cause the death?

One of the cops said, "Okay, that does it. We're going to shut down the—"

At that moment, Wilma heard a loud yell and felt someone push her roughly aside. She was about to protest when she saw who it was. Roger Anderson, Mr. Jolly Roger Enterprises himself! He did not look happy.

Roger ripped down the yellow crime-scene tape and stormed over to the cops. "What's going on here?" he roared.

"Don't you know that time is money? My men have to get back to work!"

"Now hold on," the cop said. "Right now this is a crime scene, Mr. Anderson."

Roger started to protest, but the cop shook his head. "We'll tell you when your men can come back," he said. "Meantime, I want everyone out of here so our forensics people can do their work."

Wilma hurried back to her car. She called Mel on her cell phone and told him what had happened. "I'll stick around for a little while," she said. "Maybe the forensics team will give me some more information."

"I'll go through our files here," Mel said. "Maybe we'll come across a missing persons story. After all, *anyone* could be buried out there!"

Wilma hung around for another hour. The cops were still finding more bones. By the time she left the site, half a dozen more skeletons had been unearthed.

When Wilma got back to her desk, she

called the coroner's office. One of the coroner's helpers, George Benning, was an old friend of hers from school.

"There's nothing to get so excited about," George told her. "This is not a modern crime. The bones from the cove are old bones. Old, *old* bones. We've called in an expert from the university. It looks to him like these bones have been buried for about 200 years."

"How many skeletons did you find?" Wilma asked.

"A lot," George replied. "They're still bringing in more remains."

Wilma frowned. "I thought I knew this area, George," she said. "I don't remember anyone ever mentioning an old cemetery out on the bluff."

"These bodies hadn't been buried properly, Wil," George said. "That site looks like a mass grave. Whoever buried these poor souls just dug a deep pit and dumped in their bodies."

Wilma gasped. "Do you think it was

the Wreckers?" she asked.

"Yeah. I'd be willing to bet on it," George said. "Most of the Wreckers were killed. Only a few went to prison."

"But I always thought the Wreckers' bodies had ended up buried in the town graveyard," Wilma said.

"There are no Wreckers buried in the town cemetery," George said. "Don't forget, after the battle, a lot of people who'd lost loved ones were afraid to go down to the beach."

"That's true," Wilma said. "The families were reluctant to go after their dead. They feared that the soldiers would arrest them, too. So what do you think really happened?"

"Well, it looks like the soldiers dragged the bodies up to the top of the bluff," George said. "They dug a mass grave there and tossed in the dead." He laughed. "So that means Roger's building his resort on a boneyard."

"He's building on a what?" Wilma

had never heard the word before.

"*Boneyard.* It's just another word for graveyard," George explained.

Wilma shuddered. "What an awful way to end up!" she groaned.

"Yeah, and don't forget Bloody Jack Cain's warning! *Blood in the sand,*" George added dramatically.

Wilma laughed. "I guess you must have liked the article I wrote."

"You bet," George said. "Well, now the bones have been disturbed, so to speak. So be careful, Wil. Don't let the ghost of one of those Wreckers get you."

"Very funny," Wilma said as she hung up the phone.

For a long time she stared at her computer screen, but she was thinking about what Audrey had said: "Jack warned the soldiers that people would pay for any blood that had been spilled on the sand."

Then Wilma shook her head. "Get real!" she told herself crossly. "It's time to stop stalling and get back to work."

Mel had told her to find out what the cops planned to do with the bones.

Wilma called George and explained what her boss wanted. He laughed. "You'll love this, Wil—guess who agreed to pay to have the skeletons buried in the local cemetery? Roger Anderson."

"Roger?" Wilma said. "But he's always so tight with his money! Why would he offer to do such a thing?"

"For the publicity," George answered. "I hear he's making arrangements for a ceremony to go with the burial. Won't that make a great front-page story?"

Chapter 5

Two days later, Roger's workmen were back on the job. Wilma stopped by the construction site in the middle of the afternoon, but she didn't stay long. Watching the bulldozers tearing up the bluff hurt her too much.

She was on her way back to the newsroom when she noticed a crowd outside Roger's Museum of the Macabre. She pulled over and parked. As she got out of her car, she heard someone call her name. When she turned around, she saw Donny Anderson waving at her.

"Hey," Wilma called. "What are you up to? Where's your cousin?"

"He's playing video games," Donny said. "I told him I wanted to visit the museum, but he didn't want to come with me. I don't think Steve cares very much about history."

"I'm on my way to the museum right now," Wilma said. "Would you like some company?"

Donny grinned. "Great! You can tell me what's real and what came out of Uncle Roger's fantastic imagination."

Wilma laughed. "You seem to know your uncle pretty well."

Donny nodded. "By the way, did you hear there's a brand new exhibit?"

"No," Wilma said. She glanced at the long line outside the museum. "So that's why there's such a big crowd."

"The new exhibit just opened up," Donny said. "Uncle Roger's had people working night and day to get it ready."

They paid their admission and went inside. The interior was kept very dark to make the exhibits seem scarier. Wilma could see people's shapes moving around her and hear their voices. But she couldn't make out any faces.

She and Donny followed the crowd down a long hall. The rooms of exhibits were on each side. The biggest room held the glassed-in displays of the Wreckers.

The first display showed the Wreckers moving all the warning beacons so a ship's captain would think the cove was safe. In the next display, Wreckers were shown clubbing innocent victims who were trying to swim to shore. In a third display, a cruel-looking Wrecker gleefully held up handfuls of jewels and gold coins. The body of a young sailor lay at his feet.

Donny was fascinated. "Is this the way it really was?" he asked.

"Well, sort of," Wilma said, as they stopped in front of the next glass case. Now she and Donny were gazing at the model of a fierce-looking Wrecker hiding stolen cargo in a barn. It reminded Wilma of another verse from *A Smuggler's Song*. She recited it for Donny.

"*If you see the stable-door setting open wide;*

If you see a tired horse lying down inside;

If your mother mends a coat cut about and tore;

If the lining's wet and warm—don't you ask no more!"

She grinned at Donny. "Sorry, I just couldn't resist."

"What a great poem! I'm going to have to get a copy," Donny said. "I'd like to read the whole thing."

"The trouble is," Wilma went on, "the poem and these displays make the Wreckers seem glamorous. But they weren't. They were lowdown criminals."

As they walked from one display to the next, Wilma noticed that the crowd was thinning out. It was almost closing time. The last display in the room showed several smugglers hanging from the gallows.

"Most of the Wreckers died on the beach," Wilma said. "The rest of them were eventually hunted down, put on trial, and hanged. It wasn't a very glamorous or dignified way to end a life."

Donny looked at her solemnly. "So none of the Wreckers survived," he said.

"No," Wilma said. "But, hey—how would you like to get a soda?" Wilma added. "I'm buying."

"Sure," Donny said. "Sounds good. But which display is the newest one?"

"I'd forgotten about the new one," Wilma said. "It's not in this room. Let's go see what Roger's rigged up!"

The new display—the biggest of all—was exhibited in a room by itself. It was a life-size section of the bluff at Wreckers Cove. In the foreground was a deep, ugly pit. Lying on the mounds of earth next to the pit were several skeletons the workers had dug up.

Wilma leaned close to the glass, carefully observing every detail. She was startled to see the skull with a gaping hole in its side.

"Oh, Donny!" she gasped. "What in the world has your uncle done? I thought he promised to give those bones a proper burial."

"Those aren't the *real* bones," Donny said with a laugh. "I heard Uncle Roger talking to a guy on the phone. He was arranging to have some fake bones and skulls made for the museum."

"You could have fooled me," Wilma said. "They certainly look real." She shuddered. "*Too* real," she muttered to herself.

Chapter 6

Outside the museum, a withering blast of summer heat hit Wilma and Donny like a blowtorch.

"That soda is going to taste really good," Donny said, squinting against the sunlight. "I'll ask them to serve it with a whole lot of ice."

"How about if we go to The Crow's Nest?" Wilma said. "I could use another dose of strong air-conditioning, too."

Donny laughed and said something else. But his words were drowned out by several shrill screams.

"That came from inside the museum!" he cried out.

"Come on!" Wilma pushed past the front door ticket-taker and went inside.

She paused for a moment, looking around to see who had screamed and why.

As her eyes grew used to the dark, she saw a knot of people at the far end of the hall. "Call 911!" a woman's voice yelled.

"Turn on the lights," another person said. "Someone's been hurt."

Wilma turned to Donny. "Can you get the guy at the door to give us some light?" she asked. "And tell him to call for an ambulance."

Donny nodded. Wilma hurried toward the small crowd of visitors.

"What happened?" she called out to a woman at the back of the crowd.

"I'm not sure," the woman replied. "Some lady started screaming as if she was being attacked!"

Wilma pushed through the crowd and saw a woman lying on her back, her eyes closed. A man knelt beside her, trying to revive her.

"Is she badly hurt?" Wilma asked.

The man said, "I don't think so, but—"

"An ambulance is on the way," Wilma said. "Can you tell me what happened?"

"I'm not sure," the man said. "My wife and I were talking about the display. I thought I saw someone move up behind her. I stepped to the side to give the person a better view. All of a sudden, he grabbed her and jerked her back."

"Did you get a good look at him?"

"No, that was the really weird part. He was just a shadow. And—" He frowned. "Then he just vanished."

"You mean he got away," Wilma said.

"No, I mean he *vanished*—into thin air!" The man shrugged. "I don't know how to explain it, except that he was there one second and gone the next."

At that moment the EMTs arrived. They were followed by a police officer who took the husband's story.

"I know what I'm saying sounds crazy," the man said, "but—"

"That's okay," the officer replied. "People often think they see strange things when they're suddenly put under a lot of stress."

Wilma took another look at the display the couple had been studying. It was the new exhibit, the one showing the skeletons in the sand.

Blood in the sand! Audrey's corny story came back to Wilma. She started to shiver. If those words were so corny, why did they give her chills?

All of a sudden she remembered Donny. She still owed him a soda.

As Wilma headed for the exit, her cell phone rang. It was Mel. "Where are you?" he growled.

Wilma filled him in on the new exhibit and the injured woman.

"Probably someone trying to steal her purse in the dark," Mel said. "Still, if you can tie it in with a story on that new exhibit . . ." His voice trailed away.

"You want to give Roger even more bad publicity?" Wilma said with a grin. "Okay, I'll be back in five minutes."

Donny was waiting outside.

"I'm sorry, but I have to get back to work," she told him. "Can we postpone that soda until tomorrow?"

"Oh, sure. I think I've had enough excitement for one day," Donny said. "I'm going to look for Steve. Maybe we can catch a few waves down at the cove before it gets dark."

"Be careful," Wilma warned him. "They're pretty strict about keeping people away from the construction site."

Donny nodded. "We won't go down there if they're still working," he said.

Wilma hurried to the newsroom and wrote her story. When she finished, she glanced at her watch. It was late.

As she started her car, she heard sirens. Several cop cars and an ambulance whizzed by, lights flashing.

"Oh, dear," Wilma thought. "Could be a bad accident. Maybe I'd better check it out before I go home."

She drove in the direction the cop cars

had taken. Before long she realized they were heading toward the cove. "Don't tell me something *else* has happened out there," Wilma muttered.

Sure enough, both the police cars and the ambulance turned off the highway and drove toward the bluff.

Floodlights had been turned on around the edge of the work area. Wilma could see what had happened. She just couldn't believe what she was seeing.

It looked as if a giant child had been playing with the heavy equipment. Bulldozers, trucks, and forklifts lay on their sides or upside down. Tools were scattered. The site was a disaster.

"At least it's only equipment," Wilma thought. "It can always be replaced."

Then she spotted a familiar figure standing near the ambulance. It was Donny. His face was as white as a sheet, and he was shaking from head to toe.

Chapter 7

While talking to one of the cops, Donny pointed to someone on a stretcher. Wilma's breath caught in her throat. That looked like Roger's son, Steve!

She hurried over to a cop who was stringing yellow crime-scene tape. He recognized Wilma. "Second time we've been called out here this week," he grumbled. "I sure hope this isn't going to become a habit."

"What's going on?" Wilma asked.

The cop shook his head. "You'll have to wait for the official report," he said.

"You're kidding!" Wilma cried. "What happened to the heavy equipment?"

The cop's mouth tightened. "I told you, Wilma, you'll have to wait."

Wilma sighed. "Okay, but what about the two boys? I know those kids. Please! Can't you tell me anything?"

The cop took a deep breath. "The boys are okay. Steve's got a mild concussion, but Donny's just scared. We've already called Roger. He's on his way."

At that moment, Wilma heard a familiar voice behind her. It was Roger Anderson. He pushed past Wilma and headed for the boys. A moment later he climbed into the ambulance with Steve.

"If Donny's okay, can I give him a ride home?" Wilma asked the cop.

Donny looked over at her and gave her a shaky smile. "That would be great," he said thankfully.

The cop nodded. "Okay, kid, go on home and take it easy."

"What happened out here?" Wilma asked, as she drove back to town.

"You wouldn't believe me if I told you," Donny said. "The cops didn't seem to believe me. Why should you?" He sounded frightened and angry.

"Try me," Wilma said.

Donny took a deep breath. "Okay. It was the Wreckers," he said. "I swear it was the Wreckers."

For a moment, Wilma didn't say anything. She didn't know what to say.

"I'm *not* crazy!" Donny insisted.

"I don't think you're crazy," Wilma reassured him. "But, hey—maybe you just *thought* you saw the Wreckers. Isn't that possible?"

Donny's mouth tightened. "See? You're just like everyone else. You don't really want to listen."

"Okay," Wilma said, "you're right. I'm not being fair. Tell me what happened. I promise to keep an open mind."

Donny sighed and told his story.

The boys had gone down to the cove just as the construction crew was leaving. One of the workers had warned Donny and Steve about boogie boarding so late. "It'll be dark soon," the worker had said.

45

"You kids better be real careful."

"Stay away from the work site," another man had warned. "If you two weren't related to Mr. Anderson, we'd chase you right out of here."

Donny and Steve promised to stay for only an hour. But they were having so much fun they forgot the time. The setting sun surprised them. Donny said, "We'd better get home."

Steve agreed. As they started up the path, Steve suddenly stopped. Donny almost ran into him. "What's wrong—" Donny started to say. Then he saw what had stopped Steve in his tracks.

Standing at the edge of the bluff were a dozen or more men. They were dressed in the kind of clothes worn by the figures in the museum! For a moment, Donny thought they must be local people dressed up in costumes.

"I guess Steve must have thought so, too," Donny said to Wilma. "He was worried about his dad's work site."

"Why?" Wilma asked.

"A lot of people don't want a resort built at the cove," Donny said. "Uncle Roger has gotten a few threats."

"So you saw some people. Then what did you and Steve do?" Wilma asked.

"We ran the rest of the way up the path," Donny said. "Steve had left his cell phone in the car. We were going to call his dad. But when we got to the top of the bluff—" Now Donny was breathing hard, as if the memory was upsetting him.

"Take it easy," Wilma said. "You don't have to talk about it if—"

Donny went on as if he hadn't heard her. "The Wreckers were just standing there in a group. Then, out of nowhere, a whirlwind began to blow around them. It blew harder and harder until Steve and I could hardly stand up. We dropped to the ground and just watched."

Donny's eyes widened in fear at the vivid memory.

"The equipment just started moving

by itself. The trucks, the bulldozers—all that stuff! Those big machines flew up in the air, flipped over, and fell back down. Like they were nothing!"

"So the equipment was damaged by a storm—"

"Don't you understand? *They* made it happen," Donny said angrily. "Then the Wreckers turned and looked right at us. They were grinning. Steve started to get up, but one of the men pointed his finger at him. Steve lost his balance and rolled down the path. I was scared he'd been killed. I figured I was next! But then—"

He turned and gazed at Wilma. She could tell that he really didn't see her. He was seeing something else.

"The Wreckers disappeared!" Donny said. "I swear they just *vanished*! It was like they'd never been there at all."

Chapter 8

"Okay, Donny—if you could see the Wreckers grinning," Wilma said, "they must have been standing pretty close to you. Can you describe their leader?"

Donny closed his eyes. For a moment, Wilma was afraid he wouldn't be able to answer her question.

"He was the one who made Steve fall," Donny said. "He was tall—over six feet. He had long black hair and black eyes. An ugly scar ran down the side of his face." Donny glanced at Wilma. "That's about all I remember," he said. "Except, I could have sworn that one side of his head was bleeding." He shrugged. "Okay, say it: My story sounds crazy."

"You're right," Wilma said slowly. "That is a crazy story."

"Then *you* explain it," Donny said as he folded his arms across his chest.

Wilma could feel him glaring at her, but she stared straight ahead.

"I thought you said you didn't believe in ghosts," she said at last.

"Until today I didn't believe in ghosts. But after what I saw at the cove—" he shuddered.

Wilma smiled. "Okay, I'll let you off the hook. The fact is, I do believe you."

Donny seemed surprised. "You *do*?"

Wilma nodded. "In the first place, a storm that was big enough to overturn heavy equipment would have ravaged the whole countryside. It couldn't have been a storm. In the second place, no person I know is strong enough to damage equipment like that. Thirdly, I keep remembering what that man in the museum told me about his wife's attacker—the guy just *vanished*."

She glanced at Donny and her smile widened. "Last but not least is your description of Bloody Jack Cain. I know of only one picture of him, a painting in Audrey Cain's home. You never saw it— but you described Jack perfectly."

Donny took a deep breath and let it out slowly. "You don't know how glad I am to hear you say that."

"What I don't understand," Wilma went on, "is exactly why the Wreckers have returned."

"Because their bones were disturbed," Donny said. "Isn't that always why ghosts come back to haunt people?"

"I suppose so," Wilma said, "but it still makes no sense. I thought Roger had the bones buried in the local cemetery."

Donny said nothing. Wilma glanced at him and saw that he was frowning. "What's wrong?" she asked.

"That hasn't happened yet. There's going to be a big ceremony to go along with the burial," Donny said.

Wilma gasped. That was what George had told her, too.

"I overheard Uncle Roger making the arrangements," Donny went on. "But he was scheduling the ceremony for some time next week."

At that moment Wilma remembered the skull with the hole in its side. "Donny, those bones displayed in the museum *are* the real bones! They must be."

Donny sat up straight. "You think Uncle Roger put them on display until the fake skeletons got here?"

Wilma blurted, "Why, that greedy, scheming—" Then she remembered that Donny was Roger's nephew. "Sorry," she said. "It's just that I have a hard time accepting your uncle's moral values."

"I'm sure he never thought the Wreckers would come back," Donny said. "Now what do we do?"

"I'm going to try to convince your uncle to bury those bones right away," Wilma said. "Who cares about the publicity? I have a feeling it's the only way we're going to get rid of the ghosts."

When they reached Roger's house, Donny got out of the car and burst out laughing. "Good luck," he said. "Uncle Roger may be a member of my family, but I know what he's really like. He loves attention as much as he loves money."

The housekeeper met them at the door. "Mr. Anderson's still at the hospital with Steve, but he'll be home soon."

"How's my cousin?" Donny asked.

"He'll be in the hospital overnight," the housekeeper said. "I'm on my way home. Can you take care of yourselves?"

"Sure," Donny said. He grabbed Wilma's arm. "Kitchen. Food. Okay?"

She laughed as he dragged her toward the kitchen. "Ghost-busting seems to have given you a good appetite," she said.

"We haven't busted anything yet," Donny said with a grin. "But a little food never hurt anything."

Roger's kitchen was huge. Wilma glanced at all the fancy appliances as Donny headed for the refrigerator.

"What can I do to help?" she asked.

"Maybe get us a couple of plates," Donny said. He pulled out plastic boxes, bottles, and jars from the refrigerator. "Cupboard by the sink," he added.

Wilma suddenly froze as she opened the cupboard and reached for the plates. She felt as if ice chips were trickling down her spine. "Someone is watching us," she whispered.

She glanced out the window. Had something moved in the darkness?

Closing the cupboard, she turned and switched off the kitchen light. "Close the refrigerator door," she said softly.

Donny did as he was told, and the room went dark.

"What is it?" Donny whispered.

"I think someone is looking in from outside," Wilma whispered. "*—or some thing!*" she said to herself.

Chapter 9

"Oh, don't worry," Donny said in a normal tone as he headed toward the light switch. "The dogs haven't barked, so it's probably just Uncle Roger."

But Wilma still felt those ice chips. "They didn't bark when we got here," she said, "and the dogs don't know me."

"But they know *me*," Donny said. He reached out to switch on the light, but Wilma pushed his hand aside. "Don't!" she gasped. "It's not your uncle."

"How—"

She began to recite:

"Knocks and footsteps round the house—whistles after dark—

You've no call for running out till the house-dogs bark.

Trusty's here, and Pincher's here, and

see how dumb they lie—

They don't fret to follow when the Gentlemen go by!"

Donny froze. "Are you saying that it's the Wreckers out there?"

"I'm not sure," Wilma whispered, "but yes, that's what I think."

"I thought dogs were more sensitive to ghosts than people are," Donny said.

Wilma shrugged. "I'm no expert, Donny," she whispered. "Let's wait a minute, okay? Can you see anything?"

Beyond the kitchen window, Donny could see the moon coming up. It was going to be full tonight.

Not a good night for Wreckers, Wilma thought. She knew they favored only the darkest nights.

Suddenly she saw a shadow move. Her eyes strained to see what it was. Could it be small tree branches shifting in the wind? A wild animal coming into the yard?

Another shadow moved, and then

another. Then more. Wilma's heart was pounding with fear. The shadows came together as a group, then drew apart.

"I see them!" Donny whispered.

Wilma touched Donny's hand. "We've got to get out of here," she muttered.

"Aren't we safer indoors?" he asked.

"I don't know," Wilma groaned. "What do you suppose they want?"

And then she knew! This was *Roger's* house. It was *Roger* the ghosts were after. Roger had dug up their bones and disturbed their rest. He'd put their bones on public display—a clear sign of disrespect. And Roger wanted to build a tourist resort on the site of their grave.

Roger had to die!

In a hurried whisper, she told Donny what she thought. "Call the hospital," Wilma told him. "See if you can stop your uncle before he heads back home."

She couldn't take her eyes off the shadows spreading out around the house. How many of them were there?

She wasn't sure just how many Wreckers had died at the cove two centuries ago. Fifteen? Twenty? More?

Donny slammed down the receiver. "The nurse wouldn't let me talk to him. She told me she'd take a message! When I tried to tell her about the Wreckers, she got mad. She said it wasn't funny to joke around about ghosts. She didn't believe a word I said!"

"I should have thought of that," Wilma said with a sigh. "Donny, we're on our own. No one's going to believe us. We've got to get to the museum."

She heard him draw his breath in sharply. "And do what?" he asked.

"Break in," Wilma said. "Get the bones. Sneak over to the cemetery and bury them."

Donny whistled. "Oh, *sure*! Breaking and entering—my favorite things to do." His voice sounded panic-stricken, which was exactly how Wilma felt.

"Okay, Mr. Ghost-Buster, do you have

a better idea, then?" she snapped.

"Nope." He looked discouraged.

"Cheer up," Wilma said. "It could be worse—I think. Do you know where we can find some shovels? Any flashlights?"

After adding a few more tools to the list, they raided Roger's basement and the garage.

Back in the kitchen, Donny said, "How do we get to your car?"

"Good question. Tell me, Donny, does Roger have outside lights?"

"Yeah, but how will that help?"

"I could be wrong," Wilma said, "but I'm guessing the ghosts don't do too well in the light. Remember, the inside of the museum was really dark. And the ghosts didn't show up at the construction site until the sun went down."

"That makes sense," Donny said.

Wilma nodded. "Let's turn on every outside light you've got."

"Look!" she exclaimed as the yard flooded with light. They watched as the shadow figures quickly backed into deep patches of darkness.

Wilma flung open the front door, and they ran across the lawn. As they dove into the car, a strange high-pitched howl seemed to be coming from everywhere at once. It might have been the wind—but Wilma knew it wasn't. It was the sound of pure rage.

Wilma shuddered as she put the key in the ignition and started the car.

"Did you hear that?" Donny asked, tossing the tools into the back seat.

Wilma nodded. "I have a feeling the Wreckers aren't too happy with us," she said, as they pulled away from the curb. "I sure hope they don't try to follow us."

Chapter 10

"How do you plan to get into the museum?" Donny asked as they drove into the downtown area.

"Break in through the back, I guess," Wilma said. "Do you know if there's an alarm system?"

"I don't think so," Donny said. "When Uncle Roger was ordering those fake bones, I heard him say he planned to install an alarm system. But I don't think he's done it yet."

They reached the town's main street a few minutes later. By now it was late and the street was nearly empty. Wilma drove down an alley and parked behind the museum. Donny hopped out and headed straight for the back door.

"It's a piece of cake!" he exclaimed,

fingering the padlock. "Hand me those bolt cutters, Wilma."

Wilma watched as Donny cut the lock. "You're just *way* too good with those bolt cutters," she said with a smile. "I hope I'm not starting you off on a life of crime."

Donny grinned. "Not in this lifetime!" Then, he suddenly grabbed Wilma's arm and pulled her into the shadows.

"What's the matter?" she whispered.

"A cop car just went by at the end of the alley. If they see your car—Wilma, we've got to hurry."

"Right!" She pulled a couple of big plastic trash bags out of the trunk.

"What're those for?" Donny asked.

"The bones," Wilma said. "Come on."

Once they were inside the museum, Wilma switched on a flashlight. They fumbled their way through the back rooms until they found the main hall. When they reached the showroom where the bones were exhibited, Wilma shone her light around. Before long she found the door of the display area. Donny went to work on the lock with a screwdriver.

"At least we don't have to break the glass," Wilma said. Her voice echoed in the empty room.

Once he had the door open, Donny found the light switch and flooded the exhibit with light.

Knowing these were the real bones, Wilma found she didn't want to touch them. But Donny didn't seem to mind. He began to shove the bones into one of the plastic bags.

"Careful!" Wilma cried. "Those old bones are fragile. They might break."

"Who cares?" Donny said. "I just want to get this over with."

Wilma reached for a skull. It was the one with the hole in the side. As she lifted it up, it seemed to grin at her. She suddenly remembered Audrey's story about Jack Cain. The man had been clubbed to death! Was she holding Bloody Jack Cain's skull?

"Ugh!" Wilma exclaimed as she dropped the skull into the bag and picked up another one.

"The way these skeletons were dug up," Donny said, "it's hard to tell which skulls go with which bones."

Wilma shuddered. "I really don't think it matters at this point. Let's just get the job done before—" She broke off, clamping her mouth shut.

"Before what?" Donny asked as he glanced over at her.

"Before—before either the Wreckers or the cops find us."

Donny nodded and began to work much faster.

In a few minutes they had collected all the bones and skulls. As they dragged the bags down the hall, Wilma thought she heard a creaking sound. She froze. In the darkness, Donny almost ran into her. "Listen," Wilma whispered.

They were silent and still for a minute or two. Then Donny whispered softly,

"I don't hear anything. Do you?"

"No. Maybe I just imagined I heard something," Wilma said. "I'm sorry. Guess I'm a little jumpy."

"Gee, I wonder why," Donny said as he gave her a friendly nudge.

When they found their way to the back of the museum, Wilma paused at the alley door. "I'll take a quick look around," she said. "You know—in case the cops are checking out my car."

She cracked open the door and peered through. "Everything looks okay," she said. Then she opened the door a little wider. The alley seemed to be empty.

"The coast is clear. Come on," Wilma said softly. She stepped outside.

At that moment a piercing, high-pitched howl filled the air. Wilma screamed and jumped back as shadows came swirling around her. She knocked against Donny, who was standing right behind her.

Then suddenly, the air was filled with

the disgusting odor of rotting meat. Smoky shadows blocked the light of the moon. The howl of rage grew so loud that it was almost painful.

Wilma dropped the bag and put her hands over her ears. She was more afraid than she had ever been in her life. The Wreckers were everywhere. The thick odor of death and their high-pitched screams pressed in on her. *I can't breathe*, Wilma thought. *I can't think. I can't hear.*

Then she felt someone shoving her from behind. For a moment, she thought it was one of the Wreckers.

But then she could hear a familiar voice shouting, "Move!"

It was Donny yelling at her. He grabbed the bag she had dropped and shoved her toward the car. As Wilma stumbled ahead, Donny opened the driver's side door and pushed her in.

She slid across the seat. It was as if she had entered another world! The inside of the car was quiet. Shadows pressed against the windshield—but for some reason the Wreckers couldn't get in.

Donny climbed behind the wheel, tossing the bags and tools into the back seat. He quickly slammed the door shut and locked it.

As he started the engine, Wilma wondered if he had his driver's license. Then the terrible faces came closer and began to press against every window. She remembered the damage the ghosts had done at the cove.

She decided she didn't care whether or not Donny could drive legally. All she wanted was to get out of there—*fast*.

# Chapter 11

As Donny drove down Main Street, Wilma could see that he was shaking from head to toe.

"Do you want me to drive?" she said.

"Hold up your hand," he replied.

"What?"

"Just do it," Donny snapped.

When Wilma held up her hand, it was trembling like a leaf. "Okay, so maybe I'm a little shaky, too," she admitted.

"Funny thing about ghosts. They do it to you every time," Donny said in a shaky voice. "Where's the cemetery?"

Wilma gave him directions. In another two minutes, they turned off onto a quiet side street.

Donny looked worried, and Wilma knew why! This street was poorly lit.

They parked in front of the main entrance to the cemetery. Wilma remembered what George had called this place—a boneyard! She shivered.

"There's one good thing about this cemetery," she said as they climbed out of the car. "It's not fenced in. No breaking and entering."

"It's about time our luck changed," Donny said. He pulled the shovels, flashlights, and bags of bones from the back seat. "Can you help me carry some of this stuff?"

Wilma nodded. "Do you have any idea where Roger planned to have the bones buried?" she asked.

Donny shook his head. "Does it matter?" he asked. "Can't we just pick a spot and start digging?"

"I'd like to find an out-of-the-way place," Wilma said. "I don't think what we're doing is—um, legal."

Donny glanced at his watch. "Okay, but let's make it fast. Uncle Roger is probably on his way home. I don't know if the ghosts plan to go after him or after us. But I figure we have about twenty minutes to get rid of the bones."

"Oh, great!" Wilma groaned. She glanced around. "Maybe at the back," she said, pointing.

They grabbed the bags and tools and headed across the grass toward a small clearing surrounded by trees and bushes. It wasn't likely that anyone passing by would notice them digging here. And the bright silver light of the full moon would help them see better.

Without another word, they dropped the bags and started digging. Luckily, the ground was soft in this spot. In a few minutes they'd dug down to a depth of about three feet.

"Is this deep enough?" Wilma asked. She had a big blister on one hand and a splinter in the other.

"Just a little bit deeper," Donny said. "I sure don't want those Wrecker dudes coming back to visit any time soon."

Wilma tried to ignore the pain in her hands. She kept on digging until she thought she heard something. Then she stopped and listened. There was a faint whine in the distance.

Donny had heard it, too. "Are those sirens?" he asked, leaning on his shovel for a moment.

Wilma nodded. "Yeah. They sound like they're heading toward your uncle's house," she said.

Donny took a deep breath. "We've got to get those bones in the ground *now*," he said. He tipped one of the bags onto the grass. The yellowing old bones tumbled out into the moonlight.

A skull rolled to Wilma's feet and seemed to be grinning up at her. Its empty eye sockets were black holes.

Wilma gasped. It was the skull she thought might have belonged to Jack Cain! She reached down to push it into the grave.

Suddenly, the approaching sirens were drowned out by the high-pitched howl of the ghosts.

Wilma looked up. Looming over her was a dark mass, almost like thick smoke. But as she watched, it took on the shape of a human. Then Wilma saw features forming out of the dark mass. A thin face. A scar on one cheek. Black eyes that glared at her with rage. Lips pulled back over sharp teeth locked in a terrible grin.

Bloody Jack Cain!

Wilma cried out. At the same time she heard Donny yelling. But an invisible wall was now between them! Donny couldn't get to her. Wilma was on her own.

She drew back as the ghost leaned toward her. Jack Cain's ghostly face was almost touching hers. She could smell the gruesome stink of death upon him. His bone white hands reached for her throat.

"It's not real! He's not real," Wilma told herself. But those brave words did nothing to calm her terror.

As Cain's ghostly hands came nearer, Wilma remembered the flashlight at her feet. Grabbing it and flicking it on, she directed the beam at the Wrecker's face.

He howled when the light hit him. But then the dark boiling mass slowly thinned out and disappeared.

Wilma threw the skull into the hole. "Hurry!" she cried out to Donny. "Get the rest of the bones into the ground."

Finally, they'd dumped all the bones into the hole. Then they grabbed their shovels and quickly filled it in.

At last the grave was covered. Donny dropped onto the grass. "Are we done?" he gasped.

"I think so," Wilma said, sprawling out beside him.

"What do you think? Should we say some words over the grave?" Donny asked. He looked uncertain, which was just how Wilma was feeling.

"I don't know," she said. "What can we say? Rest in peace?"

"I hope they *do* rest in peace," Donny said. "For their sake and ours."

Wilma pulled out her cell phone and handed it to Donny. "You'd better call your uncle to find out if he's okay."

Donny sat up, took the phone, and punched in some numbers. After a short conversation, he handed back the phone. "Uncle Roger's okay. He says that some burglars tried to break in. But by the time the police finally got there, the thieves had simply vanished."

"Vanished?" Wilma said.

Donny grinned. "That's what he said. *Vanished.* Can you guess why he thinks they were thieves?"

Wilma shook her head.

"Because they stole the Wreckers' bones from the museum," Donny said. He was trying hard not to laugh.

Wilma chuckled. "You mean the so-called 'fake' bones?"

Donny's grin widened. "I asked my uncle about that. But he suddenly had a bad coughing spell and had to hang up."

Wilma smiled. "I'm glad it's over," she said, climbing to her feet.

"It really *is* over, isn't it?" Donny asked, his face suddenly serious.

"I hope so," Wilma said. "As long as those bones stay buried, I think we're okay. But if someone ever decides to find out what's under that patch of dirt—" Her voice trailed away.

Donny shrugged. "But next time, I'll know just what to do," he said. He grinned and began to quote.

"Them that asks no questions isn't told a lie. Watch the wall, my darling, while the Gentlemen go by!"

COMPREHENSION QUESTIONS

RECALLING DETAILS

1. Who wrote the poem Wilma recited to Donny?

2. Where did Wilma's friend George Benning work?

3. How did Wilma's boss at the newspaper feel about Roger Anderson?

VOCABULARY

1. What's the difference between *descendants* and *ancestors*?

2. Which museum exhibit could be described as *macabre*—a famous portrait or a shrunken head? Explain why.

DRAWING CONCLUSIONS

1. Why were the Wreckers' ghosts so angry at Roger Anderson?

2. Why did Wilma let Donny drive her car without asking if he had a driver's license?